First Ladies

Barbara Bush

Joanne Mattern

ABDO
Publishing Company

visit us at
www.abdopublishing.com

Published by ABDO Publishing Company, 8000 West 78th Street, Edina, Minnesota 55439.
Copyright © 2008 by Abdo Consulting Group, Inc. International copyrights reserved in all
countries. No part of this book may be reproduced in any form without written permission from
the publisher. The Checkerboard Library™ is a trademark and logo of ABDO Publishing
Company.

Printed in the United States.

Cover Photo: Corbis
Interior Photos: Corbis pp. 5, 21, 23; Courtesy George Bush Presidential Library pp. 6, 9, 10, 11,
    12, 13, 15, 17, 18, 19, 24, 25, 26, 27; Getty Images pp. 4, 7, 20, 22, 31

Series Coordinator: BreAnn Rumsch
Editors: Megan M. Gunderson, BreAnn Rumsch
Art Direction & Cover Design: Neil Klinepier

Library of Congress Cataloging-in-Publication Data

Mattern, Joanne, 1963-
  Barbara Bush / Joanne Mattern.
     p. cm. -- (First ladies)
  Includes index.
  ISBN-13: 978-1-59928-790-4
  1. Bush, Barbara, 1925---Juvenile literature. 2. Presidents' spouses--United States--Biography--
Juvenile literature. I. Title.
  E883.B87M38 2007
  973.928092--dc22
  [B]

                                                                        2007009724

Contents

Barbara Bush

Barbara Bush is part of an important political family. She became First Lady in 1989. Her husband, George H.W. Bush, was the forty-first president of the United States. Mrs. Bush is also the mother of the forty-third president, George W. Bush.

Barbara Bush's loyalty to her husband and family made her a trustworthy First Lady.

Mrs. Bush was a popular First Lady. Many people felt she was like a grandmother to the nation. Mrs. Bush enjoyed meeting the American people. She was always friendly and warm.

But, Mrs. Bush's years as First Lady are only part of her life story. Mrs. Bush is a strong supporter of her family. And, she is known for promoting **literacy**. Mrs. Bush continues to volunteer for causes that are important to her. Her work has helped many Americans lead better lives.

Barbara Bush is proud of her family and her country.

Daddy's Little Girl

Barbara Pierce was born on June 8, 1925, in New York City, New York. The Pierce family lived in the nearby town of Rye. Barbara's parents were Marvin and Pauline Pierce. Marvin was a successful businessman. Pauline cared for their home.

Barbara had an older brother and sister. Martha, the oldest, liked to play many games with Barbara. The girls were close. But, their brother James liked to tease them.

In 1930, the Pierce family grew. The children now had a younger brother named Scott. He was often sick, so Pauline spent much of her time caring for him. This made Barbara feel ignored. So, she spent a lot of time with her father instead.

Barbara enjoyed many special moments with her father. Sometimes, Marvin took Barbara with him when he traveled for business. They also enjoyed telling jokes and funny stories. And, Marvin taught Barbara to enjoy sports.

Marvin Pierce

6

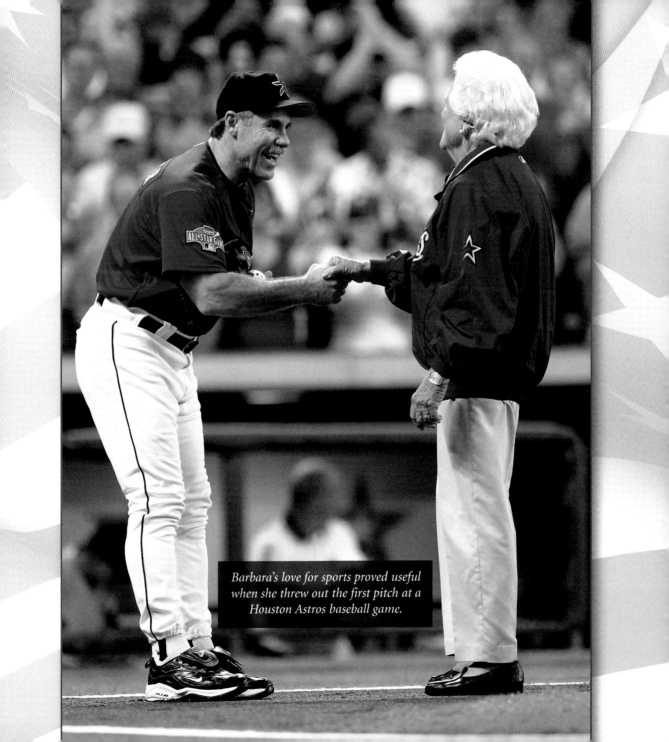

Barbara's love for sports proved useful when she threw out the first pitch at a Houston Astros baseball game.

A Happy Childhood

Barbara liked growing up in Rye. The Pierce home was in a prominent neighborhood there. Barbara loved playing in the large yard. It had several gardens and a pond. There, Barbara's father built a tree house for her brothers. Barbara liked to climb up and play in it, too.

Barbara received an excellent education. She attended the local Milton School through sixth grade. In 1938, Barbara transferred to Rye Country Day School, a private school near her home.

Like most other children in her town, Barbara also took dance lessons. Every week, she got dressed up and went to the class. However, there were too many girls and not enough boys. So, Barbara often danced the boy's role instead!

Early on, books became a very special part of Barbara's life. The Pierce home was filled with books. Everyone in the family loved to read. Barbara also enjoyed listening to stories on the radio and playing dress-up and make-believe.

By the time she was 12 years old, Barbara was taller than most of the boys her age.

One Special Boy

When Barbara was 16, her parents sent her to Ashley Hall. Ashley Hall was a girls' boarding school in South Carolina. There, Barbara liked learning science, art, and languages. She also appeared in school plays and was active in sports.

In 1941, 16-year-old Barbara went home to Rye for Christmas vacation. One night, she went to a dance. One of her friends introduced her to a boy named George Bush. George was one year older than Barbara. He also went to a private school.

Barbara and George did not spend much time together that night. But later, Barbara told her mother about the nice boy she had met. Barbara thought George was very cute.

Barbara blossomed at Ashley Hall. Friends recall her being outgoing, athletic, and very pretty.

The next night, Barbara went to another dance and George was there! The pair talked and danced together. When they went back to school, they wrote each other long letters. Soon, Barbara and George were in love.

When Barbara met George, he was a student at Phillips Academy in Andover, Massachusetts, where he played baseball.

War and Love

In 1941, the United States entered **World War II**. George wanted to help. So after graduating from high school in 1942, he joined the U.S. Navy. He went to Texas to train as a pilot.

Meanwhile, Barbara was busy too. She graduated from Ashley Hall in 1943. Then, she attended Smith College in Massachusetts. Smith was a renowned women's college. Barbara enjoyed her time there. In addition to her studies, Barbara was a member of the soccer team. She also had many friends, but she missed George terribly.

During the summer of 1943, Barbara and George had become engaged. But, they did not tell their families until Christmas. After the holidays, George was sent overseas to fight in the war. Meanwhile, Barbara went back to school. The couple exchanged many letters while George was away.

George missed the original wedding date because his plane was shot down over the Pacific Ocean.

Barbara and George planned to get married in December 1944. Barbara also decided to leave college to be a homemaker. However, George was unable to come home from the war in December. Finally, they married on January 6, 1945. Barbara was about to begin a new life.

Barbara was relieved when George came home. Their wedding reception took place at the Apawamis Club in Rye, where they had first met.

On the Road

The **newlyweds** were not able to settle down right away. Mr. Bush was still in the navy. So for eight months, the couple moved from one naval air base to another. When they did not see each other for many weeks, Mrs. Bush felt lonely.

In 1945, **World War II** ended. Now, Mr. Bush was ready to go to college. He attended Yale University in New Haven, Connecticut. The Bushes lived in a tiny apartment near the school. Mrs. Bush managed the household while her husband studied hard. On July 6, 1946, they welcomed their first child. They named their son George Walker.

Mr. Bush graduated from Yale in 1948. Then, he and Mrs. Bush decided to move to Texas. Mr. Bush had heard about many opportunities there. He got a job in the oil business.

At first, Mrs. Bush was nervous about the move. Texas was very different from New York and Connecticut! And, she would miss her family back in Rye. But, she was happy to be with her husband and their young son. Soon, they were expecting another baby.

Mrs. Bush spent her time in New Haven caring for the apartment and baby George. She also kept score for her husband's college baseball team.

Family Tragedies

In 1949, Mrs. Bush received terrible news. Her mother had been killed in a car accident. Mrs. Bush was shocked and sad. She missed her mother very much. On December 20, the couple's second child was born. They named their daughter Pauline Robinson, or Robin, after Mrs. Bush's mother.

Soon afterward, Mr. Bush started his own oil company. Around that time, the family moved into their first house in Midland, Texas. In 1953, Mrs. Bush had another baby boy named John Ellis, or Jeb. The Bush family thought their hard times were over.

However, tragedy soon struck again. In 1953, little Robin became very sick with **leukemia**. Mr. and Mrs. Bush took her to the best doctors. They even went to a special hospital in New York City. But three-year-old Robin died just eight months later.

Mrs. Bush was heartbroken after Robin died. But, she felt better when she spent time with her husband and their sons. Eventually, the Bushes had three more children. Neil was born in 1954, and Marvin was born in 1956. Finally, Dorothy was born in 1959.

The Bushes learned to lean on each other in times of tragedy. Mrs. Bush once said that "because of Robin, George and I love every living human more."

Entering Politics

By 1966, Mr. Bush was a successful businessman. But, he was also interested in politics. That year, he was elected to the U.S. House of Representatives. So, the Bushes moved to Washington, D.C.

Mrs. Bush wanted to help her husband with his job. She tried to meet all the other representatives and their wives. She and the other political wives did volunteer work together. Mrs. Bush also attended lots of meetings.

The Bush family proudly stands outside of the U.S. Capitol in Washington, D.C.

Still, Mrs. Bush made time for her family. She took the children to museums. And, they visited all the monuments in the city. One day, Mrs. Bush even took Dorothy to visit the White House.

In 1971, Mr. Bush became the U.S. ambassador to the **United Nations**. So, the family moved to New York City. Mr. and Mrs. Bush traveled to many countries to meet government officials. They even lived in China from 1974 to 1975, when Mr. Bush was head of a U.S. government office there.

When Mr. and Mrs. Bush lived in Beijing, China, they rode bicycles to get around the city.

The Second Family

In 1976, Mr. Bush was offered another government job. President Gerald Ford asked him to run the **Central Intelligence Agency**. Once again, Mr. and Mrs. Bush moved to Washington, D.C.

In 1979, Mr. Bush decided to run for president of the United States. He and Mrs. Bush worked very hard. However, the nomination went to Ronald Reagan instead. Mr. Reagan then asked Mr. Bush to be his **running mate**. They won the election in 1980! Four years later, they were reelected.

At first, Mrs. Bush was shy about speaking in public. But soon, she grew to enjoy meeting the people she and her husband wanted to help. Throughout Mr. Bush's vice presidency, Mrs. Bush stayed very busy. She and the vice president traveled to 68 countries

Barbara enjoyed her duties as Second Lady, from visiting charities to lighting the national Christmas tree.

With 59 percent of the popular vote, the Reagans and the Bushes easily won their 1984 reelection campaign.

and all 50 states. In Washington, D.C., the Bushes hosted more than 1,000 parties and dinners at their home.

At the same time, Mrs. Bush worked hard to encourage **literacy** for all Americans. She visited hundreds of schools to read to children. And, she encouraged families to make reading a part of their daily lives. Mrs. Bush also wrote a book about her dog C. Fred called *C. Fred's Story*. The book raised almost $100,000! Mrs. Bush gave all of the money to literacy organizations.

Stepping Up

In 1988, Mr. Bush ran for president. This time, he won! So in 1989, Mrs. Bush became America's First Lady. She felt ready for this position. After all, she had been the vice president's wife for eight years.

The First Lady continued to support her husband. She and the president traveled all over the United States. They met government leaders from around the world. And, they attended meetings to discuss many important issues.

Vice President and Mrs. Bush enjoyed many exciting parades during the presidential campaign.

Many people liked Mrs. Bush. They enjoyed her sense of humor. And, they appreciated her honesty. Mrs. Bush said and did what she wanted. She said she was "everybody's grandmother."

However, not everyone liked the First Lady's style. Some people thought she was old-fashioned. But Mrs. Bush did not care. She knew that supporting her husband was what she cared about most. She once said, "I always thought that one should do the best one can. I did my own thing as First Lady and I think I did it well."

Mrs. Bush's popularity helped her husband win, but so did her unwavering support. Someone once yelled out that they loved her, and she replied, "I want you to love George."

Reading and Writing

As First Lady, Mrs. Bush had the chance to make America better. She decided to continue her campaign to improve **literacy**. Mrs. Bush felt that many problems, such as **unemployment** and crime, could be solved if more people could read and write.

Mrs. Bush loved reading to children in the White House library.

In 1989, Mrs. Bush started the Barbara Bush Foundation for Family Literacy. This organization gives money to family literacy projects. The First Lady wanted everyone to know that reading was important and also fun. So, she visited schools and organizations all over the country to spread her message.

In 1989, Mrs. Bush made a special guest appearance on Sesame Street.

A Solid Foundation

On March 6, 1989, Mrs. Bush launched the Barbara Bush Foundation for Family Literacy at a White House luncheon. She said, "Sharing the pleasure of learning to read has to be one of the most important experiences a loving adult and child can have. Reading together brings families together."

The foundation works to encourage literacy in every American family. To accomplish this, the foundation teaches parents to read to their children early and often. It also helps families that have a hard time reading. And, the foundation publishes materials that show parents and teachers how to help children learn to read.

Furthermore, Mrs. Bush began an annual fundraiser in 1995 called A Celebration of Reading. There, famous authors read aloud from their books. This event raises money to help other literacy programs. As of September 2006, there were more than 500 programs in 47 states. The programs had received $17 million in aid from the foundation.

During her school visits, many children asked Mrs. Bush what it was like to live in the White House. To answer their questions, she wrote *Millie's Book*. Millie was the Bush family's dog. In the book, Millie describes life at the White House. The story is funny and interesting. Mrs. Bush's book earned more than $800,000 for her **literacy** foundation.

Home to Texas

All the Bush children married and had children of their own.
Mr. and Mrs. Bush have 14 grandchildren in all!

In 1992, President Bush ran for reelection. This time, he faced a tough opponent named Bill Clinton. The president was disappointed when Mr. Clinton won the election. But, Mrs. Bush was ready to lead a quiet life.

So, the couple moved to Houston, Texas. There, they focused on their family. Mr. and Mrs. Bush enjoyed spending time with their children and grandchildren. They enjoyed time together, too.

In 1997, Mrs. Bush helped her husband open the George Bush Presidential Library and Museum in College Station, Texas. The library houses special documents and gifts from their years in the White House.

Then in 2000, their son George W. was elected as the forty-third president of the United States. Now, Americans called Mrs. Bush the First Mother! She was very proud of her family.

Mrs. Bush liked being the First Lady because she enjoys

Volunteering remains an important part of Mrs. Bush's life. Here, she helps prepare lunch for homeless people at Martha's Table in Washington, D.C.

helping others. She continues to volunteer for many causes, such as helping **cancer** patients. She also gives speeches and hosts events to raise money for **literacy**. And, she contributes to volunteer programs in schools and communities. Barbara Bush will always be remembered as a compassionate First Lady.

Timeline

1925	Barbara Pierce was born on June 8.
1938–1941	Barbara attended Rye Country Day School.
1941–1943	Barbara attended Ashley Hall.
1943–1944	Barbara attended Smith College.
1945	Barbara married George H.W. Bush on January 6.
1946	The Bushes' son George Walker was born.
1949	The Bushes' daughter Pauline Robinson, or Robin, was born.
1953	The Bushes' son John Ellis, or Jeb, was born; their daughter Robin died.
1954	The Bushes' son Neil was born.
1956	The Bushes' son Marvin was born.
1959	The Bushes' daughter Dorothy was born.
1966	Mr. Bush was elected to the U.S. House of Representatives.
1981–1989	Mr. Bush served as Ronald Reagan's vice president.
1989–1993	Mrs. Bush acted as First Lady, while her husband served as president.
1989	Mrs. Bush started the Barbara Bush Foundation for Family Literacy.
2000	The Bushes' son George W. Bush was elected president.

Did You Know?

As a teenager, Barbara was called "Barbi." As an adult, her nickname changed to "Bar."

Mrs. Bush is related to Franklin Pierce, the fourteenth president of the United States.

Mrs. Bush's hair turned white when she was only 28, during her daughter Robin's illness.

The Bushes moved 29 times before Mr. Bush became president!

One of Mrs. Bush's favorite activities is gardening.

In addition to *C. Fred's Story* and *Millie's Book*, Mrs. Bush has written two books about her life. They are called *Barbara Bush: A Memoir* and *Reflections*.

The Bushes call their grandchildren "the Grands."

When the Bushes' son George W. was elected president, their son Jeb was serving as governor of Florida.

Barbara Bush and Abigail Adams are the only two women in American history to be both married to and the mother of a president.

Glossary

cancer - any of a group of often deadly diseases characterized by an abnormal growth of cells that destroys healthy tissues and organs.

Central Intelligence Agency - the U.S. government organization that deals with foreign matters related to national security.

leukemia - a type of cancer that affects a person's blood cells.

literacy - the state of being able to read and write.

newlywed - a person who just married.

running mate - a candidate running for a lower-rank position on an election ticket, especially the candidate for vice president.

unemployment - the state of being without a job. It is also the number of people in a country who do not have jobs.

United Nations - a group of nations formed in 1945. Its goals are peace, human rights, security, and social and economic development.

World War II - from 1939 to 1945, fought in Europe, Asia, and Africa. Great Britain, France, the United States, the Soviet Union, and their allies were on one side. Germany, Italy, Japan, and their allies were on the other side.

Web Sites

To learn more about Barbara Bush, visit ABDO Publishing Company on the World Wide Web at **www.abdopublishing.com**. Web sites about Barbara Bush are featured on our Book Links page. These links are routinely monitored and updated to provide the most current information available.

Index